The Long Road

The Long Road

by Luis Garay

Tundra Books

Published in Canada by Tundra Books
McClelland & Stewart Young Readers
481 University Avenue
Toronto, Ontario M5G 2E9

Published in the United States by Tundra Books of Northern New York,
P.O. Box 1030, Plattsburgh, N.Y. 12901

Library of Congress Catalog Number: 97-60482

Canadian Cataloguing in Publication Data

Garay, Luis, 1965-
    The long road

ISBN 0-88776-408-8

I. Title.

PS8563.A598L66 1997   jC813'.54   C97-930631-0
PZ7.G37Lo 1997

We acknowledge the support of the Canada Council for the Arts for our publishing program.

Design: Sari Ginsberg

Printed and bound in Canada

1 2 3 4 5 6   02 01 00 99 98 97

To the memory of Gordon Montador

"Come home, José!" cried Mama. The dark was coming – he could barely see the baseball as it flew through the sky.

"Don't let the door slam. Wash your hands and face, *muchacho*; it's time to eat. I want to feed you all before I go to the meeting." José grumbled but he didn't mean it. He didn't really mind coming home, or even washing.

His Uncle Ramón was telling a story: "There was a passenger on the bus, a fellow with a knapsack, come all the way from North America. . ." Uncle Ramón drove the bus everyday over the mountain to the market in the center of the city. "Here, Pinto," he called the dog and checked to see if José's aunts weren't looking. He dropped a piece of meat.

"Did you hear any news?" asked Tia Rosa. "With Christmas coming, the radio plays nothing but carols all day." Rosa and Tia Mariá worked in a store in the city.

The stories his aunts and uncle told always made José long to see the busy city, the town beyond the mountain and, most of all, the long and dusty road leading there.

"We have a surprise for you, José." His mother put down her mop and winked at her sisters. "Tomorrow you're going on the bus."

The day before Christmas was hot and dry. José was as clean as he had ever been. Mama had insisted. He wore his best T-shirt and pants.

When Uncle Ramón saw them, he grinned. "You'll be going across the mountain today, *chico*. That's a long way. Do you have all your bags?" The bags were full of gifts for Grandmother. Packed carefully in one of them was a ceramic bowl José had made by himself in school. It was yellow with pink flowers and had his name carefully printed on the bottom.

"Welcome, welcome, my little one, not so little anymore." Grandmother's house was full of the warm, spicy smell of cake. José knew there would be ice cream to eat with the cake, and ice water to drink with it.

"Grandma, I went to see a movie. There were robots in it and . . . " He told her the plot. Grandma seldom went to movies. "And you should see me play baseball," he continued, "You won't believe how much better I am." He described every inning of his last game.

"That's lovely, dear," Grandmother nodded with a smile.

On Christmas Eve as José snuggled into the spare-room bed at Grandma's house, he closed his eyes and felt as though he couldn't be happier.

A few days later, the bus let them off at the crossroads near their village. As they neared home, José strained to hear the familiar voices of the boys at the baseball diamond. No sound came. No radios, not even barking dogs.

"You there!" Both José and his mother jumped at the noise.

"Is that you, Señor Martínez?" Mama squinted into the afternoon sun. The old man approached. "What in the world has happened?"

"Soldiers came. Everyone has left. Nobody has stayed."

José thought about Uncle Ramón and his aunts, and Pinto. 'Where were they?'

"What about you, Señor? Why haven't you gone too?" Mama cried.

"I am too old to start a new life. I belong to this place." Softly he spoke, almost to himself, "Every picture inside my house fell down from the gunfire, even the one of my dear wife." Then, in a voice that was more urgent than José had ever heard, he said, "Señora Moreno, leave. Take this boy and go. And do not tell me where."

The next few days were a blur. José remembered little; his mind could only hold Uncle Ramón, his aunts, Pinto. He prayed that they were safe. He had felt this awful empty way before, when his father had been taken away to prison. They had heard nothing from him since.

José and his mother walked from one town to another, always at night and always moving north. They took shelter with friends, in a church, even in a shack full of feathery chickens. Finally came the day when Mama said, "We are near the border."

At the border was a small barn, and in its doorway stood a soldier with his rifle, as still as if he were made of wood. Minutes, time without measure, passed. José, his mother and the soldier were frozen as if in a painting. When darkness came, the boy and the woman turned away and crept over the border, following a ditch by the side of the road.

Once they were safely across they took a bus, another bus, and then another to the city. José's mother had an address written on a piece of paper. They asked directions and walked there. The building looked enormous to José. A guard stopped them at the door, but when José's mother spoke to him, he waved them inside.

Two men sat behind a desk. One of them asked questions so rapidly that José's mother hardly had time to answer. "Where is the boy's father now?" he asked her. She looked at José and back at the man. "He was in prison, but we haven't had word since his arrest." There were no more questions. The man handed her an envelope full of papers.

"God go with you" he said kindly.

Once they had their papers ready, they took another bus to the airport. When the time came to leave, Mama held his hand so tightly that her knuckles were white.

"Don't be frightened, José." It sounded as if she were speaking to herself, "The plane is big and sturdy, you'll see. Would you like to sit by the window?"

"No, thanks." The plane rolled forward and, with a roar, rose into the sky. He stared straight ahead and didn't see the green, green land disappear under the clouds.

A round-faced boy in the seat in front of him bobbed up. He spoke in a kind voice, but José didn't understand the words.

The plane landed at twilight at an airport where everything was gray: the asphalt, the buildings, everything. Mama seemed frightened, more frightened than she had been of the soldier and his rifle at the border. "Don't speak to the officers unless you are spoken to," she cautioned.

'No fear of that,' José thought. He remembered the soldier too. But all of a sudden he wondered, 'What if they don't speak Spanish?' There were so many things he wanted to know. 'Will I sleep in a bed tonight? What will I eat?' An odd thought came to him: 'This hall is as big as our baseball diamond at home.'

The men asked many questions. A translator turned their strange sounds into familiar words. They wanted to know about the fighting in the countryside, about the meetings his mother attended, and about his father's disappearance. Finally, their questions stopped. One of them smiled at José. "Welcome," he said, then, "Next!" as he turned to face the person waiting in line.

José and his mother carried their few bags into the airport arrivals level. There was no one there to meet them. They stood silently. José had never felt more desolate. He could only think; 'I have no home. I have no friends.'

"It's time to find the bus. The translator has given me an address where we can stay."

"I thought we were finished with buses," José grumbled as he loaded their few bags into its side compartment. The bus took José and his mother to a big building far away from the airport. A lady met them at the door and, with a brisk step, led them down an endless hallway.

"You'll sleep in here. I'm afraid we're rather crowded at the moment. Take any bed that's free." She waved at a room lined with cots along each wall. The light was harsh and the noise! Babies wailed and people chattered as if they had been silent for ages. José felt like they were on a strange sort of vacation.

"Do you think we should unpack, Mama?"

"No, not yet. Just take out the things you need for tonight. But soon, dear, soon."

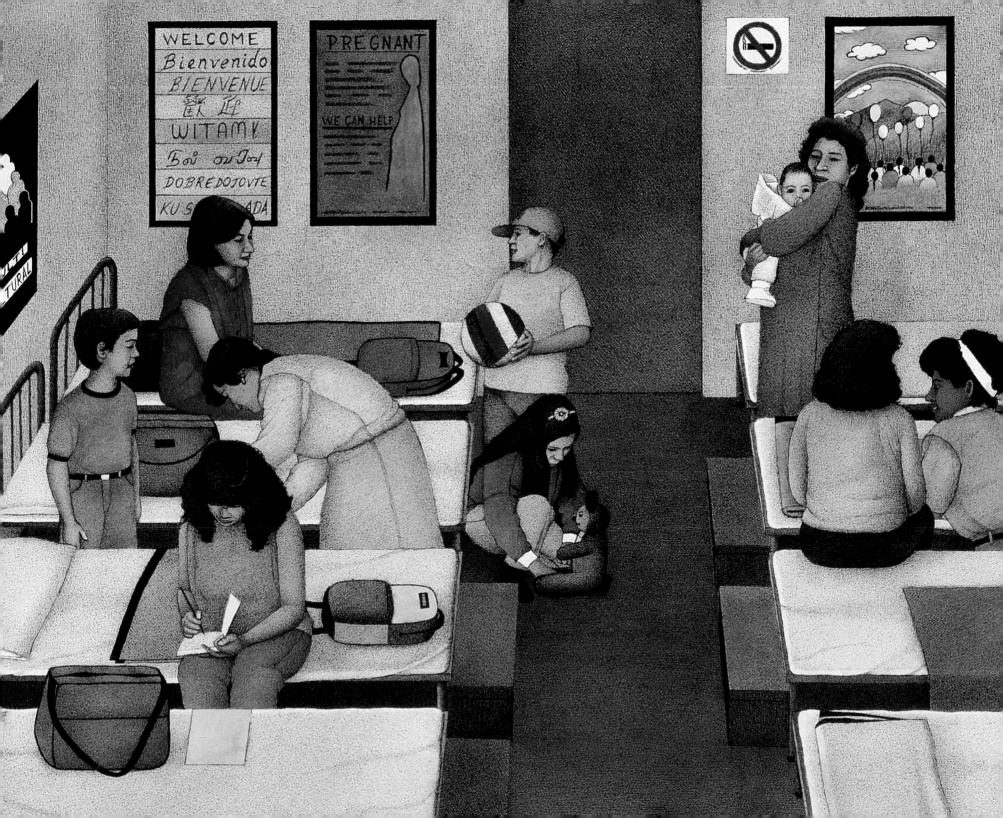

The lady at the shelter helped José's mother find a job. During the day she studied English. In the afternoon she changed clothes, and she and José went to a big building to clean offices. José liked to go with Mama. It was easier to talk there than at the noisy shelter. Every night, he practiced new English words with her.

One evening came the news José had longed to hear. "You'll never guess, José. We've found a place to live." José was relieved. Most of the others on their flight had already left the shelter and new people were arriving everyday.

"Will I be able to hang pictures on the walls?"

"Of course, and we'll make you a desk because now you will start school."

"And will we have a dog?" He thought of Pinto. Uncle Ramón had always said that every home needed a good roof and a good dog.

"We'll see."

They moved into the apartment on an icy Saturday morning. The shelter lady had given them a piece of paper and a map. "Mrs. Moreno, this is where the food depot is. You can get some basic supplies there, and some warmer clothes. You'll need them." Once José would have expected to hear his mother say no. But she thanked the woman warmly and smiled, "Thank you!"

At the depot it was José who spoke to the man. It felt strange for him to arrange things instead of Mama, but she still stumbled over almost every English word. José helped load their cart with foods that were no longer so strange: potatoes, apples, even cereal.

He had a thought: "Mama, you'll be cooking in our own kitchen tonight!"

"And on Monday, my boy, you will be going to school."

There was a time when such news would have made José sorry. But now he was very glad.

On Monday morning, he was no longer glad. "What if they don't like me? What if nobody understands what I say?"

"Your English is fine. And they will like you, José, once they get to know you. Hurry or we'll both be late." Mama helped him zip up the bulky unfamiliar jacket and shooed him out the door. His boots squeaked on the packed snow.

"Students, I would like you to meet José. He has come a long way to join us. Perhaps you could mark your journey on the map?" He saw that the map was covered in many lines, some shorter, and some much longer than his would be.

The teacher spoke so clearly and so gently that he had no trouble understanding.

By lunchtime he was no longer so frightened. He had already spoken to one or two children.

That night as they worked side by side emptying bins and mopping halls, José's mother asked him how things went.

"I think we've come a very long way, Mama. I looked at the map."

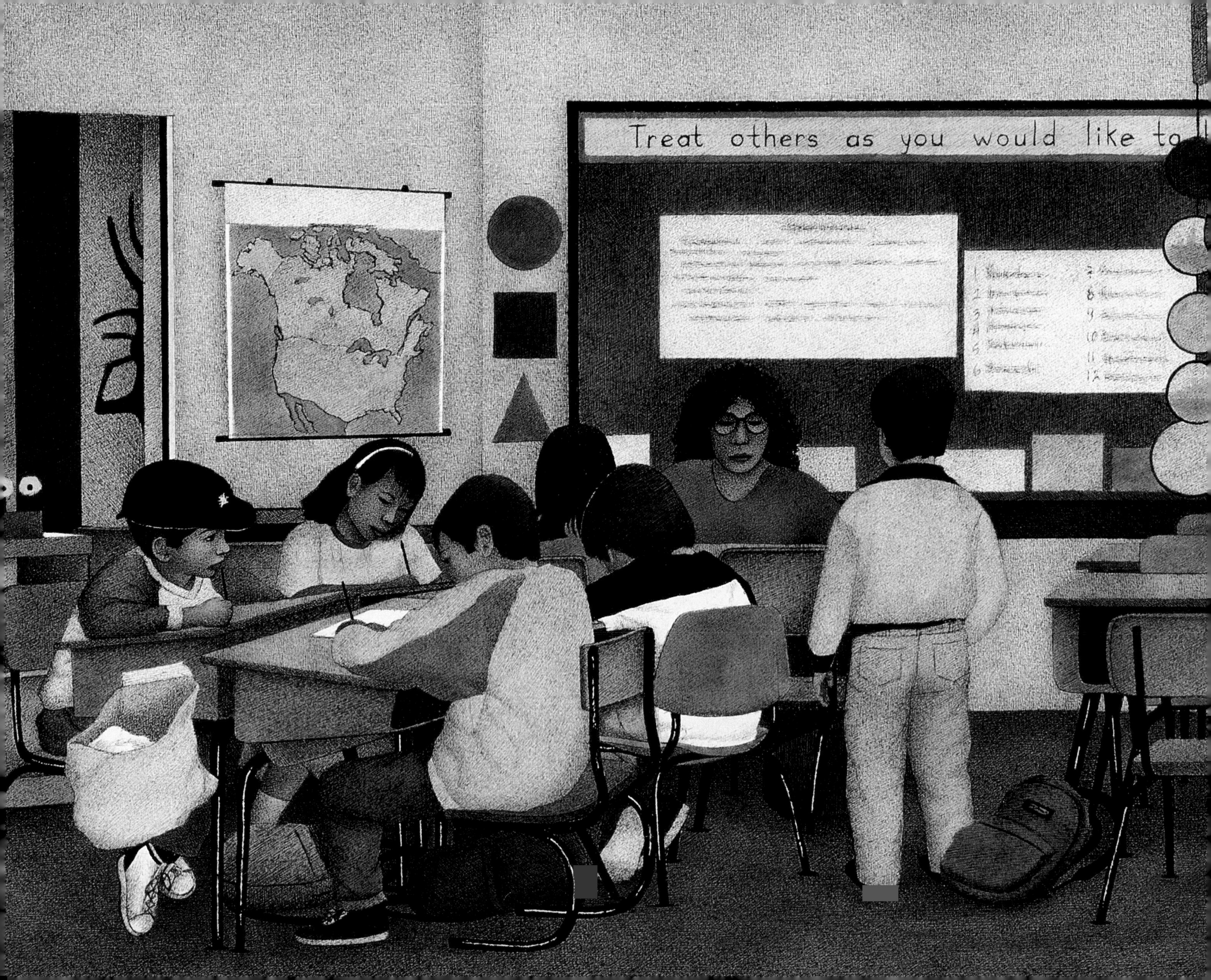
Treat others as you would like to

Soon a week passed, and then another. The strange faces in the classroom became familiar. José's English improved even more. The cold seemed less bitter. It was almost time for his birthday.

José's birthday fell on a Saturday. His mother didn't say a word about it, but José knew she would not forget. Just before lunch she said, "Get your coat. We're going out." José knew what was coming, but he pretended to be surprised for Mama's sake.

Soon they reached Teresa's house. They had met her at the shelter — it seemed like a long time ago — and she had become a friend to them both.

The door flew open. Everyone cried, "Happy Birthday, José." José was greeted by a sweet smell, the mix of cake spices and ginger he remembered from Grandmother's. For a minute he closed his eyes. He was swept up by the aroma, and by the Spanish voices he did not need to strain to understand. For a moment he thought his heart would break.

"José, isn't this just like being at home?"

One of the smaller children swung at a piñata full of candies. There appeared to be no present for him. He tried to look as if he didn't mind.

"José, your present . . ." Before José could wonder what she meant, the doorbell chimed.

"Can José come out to play? There's enough snow to make a snow-man." They were boys from school. José knew that Mama must have invited them specially. He hesitated. José had never made a snowman before. He looked at his mother.

"I think you'd better go outside. Your present needs a bit of fresh air." The others laughed. As he went to the closet to put on his boots, José heard a familiar scratching and snuffling coming from inside. It was the kind of sound he remembered well from home. He held his breath and opened the closet. Without meaning to, he cried out.

Mama smiled. "We found a dog for our new home," she said. The rest of what she said, about the walks and the feeding, was a happy hum in his ears.

The snow fell quietly as José and his friends built their snowman and played with the dog. For the very first time, José felt that the long road that had led him here could be a road to happiness he had not known since an evening long ago in the kitchen of his Uncle Ramón.